This Book Belongs to

. . . .

For the real Lulu,
who helped me imagine this story.

First published in Great Britain in 2008 by Andersen Press Ltd.,
20 Vauxhall Bridge Road, London SW1V 2SA.
Published in Australia by Random House Australia Pty.,
Level 3, 100 Pacific Highway, North Sydney, NSW 2060.
Copyright © Andy Ellis, 2008
The rights of Andy Ellis to be identified as the author and illustrator
of this work have been asserted by him in accordance with the
Copyright, Designs and Patents Act, 1988.
All rights reserved. Colour separated in Switzerland by Photolitho AG, Zürich.
Printed and bound in Singapore by Tien Wah Press.

10   9   8   7   6   5   4   3   2   1

British Library Cataloguing in Publication Data available.

ISBN 978 1 84270 753 1 (paperback)
ISBN 978 1 84270 727 2 (hardback)

This book has been printed on acid-free paper

Lulu's House   Zoo

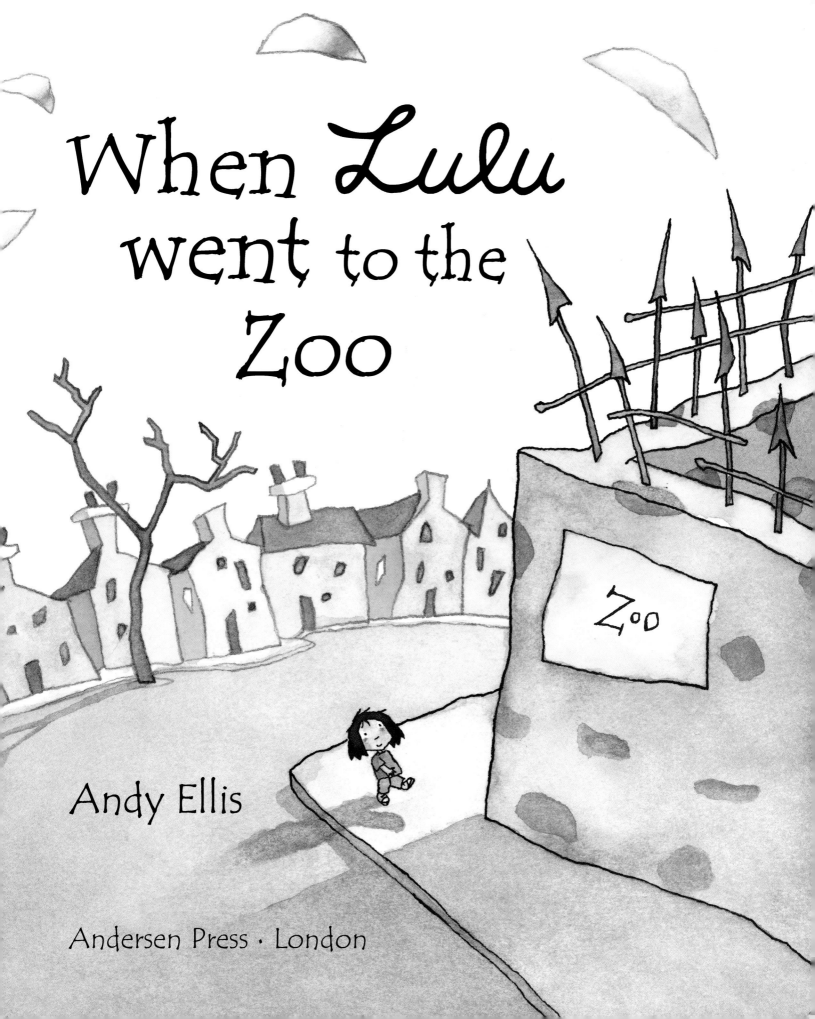

When *Lulu* went to the Zoo

Andy Ellis

Andersen Press · London

When Lulu went to the zoo...

she was sad for the giraffes
and the penguins too.

The tigers were crying really big tears
and the life had gone out of the llamas' ears.

Though Lulu was only two times two,
she knew that animals should not be in a zoo.

And though Lulu was the size
that Lulu should be,

she found that she might
(though it was a bit tight)

fit through the bars
of the cages with ease

and chat to the animals
as she swung through the trees.

She had to be careful
so nobody saw.
Then she slipped out again
through the little cage door.

And what she discovered,
while she talked to them all,

was they dreamed of splashing in a real waterfall.
Or dancing on icebergs that filled up the sea.

Or flying in the sky, flamingo or bee.

In short, to know how it feels to be free.

She whispered to the animals,
"You can come to my house.
There's room for you all,
from elephant to mouse."

And one moonless night she let them all go
and smuggled them back so no one would know.

And they lived with *sweet Lulu* in *sweet Lulu's* house.

But there wasn't **quite** room for elephant and mouse.

The fridge was too full of penguins and seals.
There was no room for food, so no one had meals.

And the bathroom was the right place
for a lovely hot wash.

But the bear in the bathtub
was a bit of a squash.

Though Lulu loved them
with a love very deep,
it was never an easy
secret to keep.

"We've found you!"
the six sad zoo-men said.
"Please give back our animals,
we'll put them to bed."

But Lulu was bold and she said, "Don't you see?
The zoo's not the place for my best friends to be.
Every one of them says they just want to be free."

And she talked,
as only a four year old can,
of an idea she had
that was called Lululand.

Lulu and the zoo-men
imagined a place
where each of the animals
had oodles of space.

Now whenever she wants to
she tiptoes away,
to visit her friends and play there all day...

...but on warm, moonlit nights
she invites them all back,
when no one is looking,

for a BIG midnight snack!

MORE ANDERSEN PRESS PAPERBACK PICTURE BOOKS

I'M COMING TO GET YOU!
by Tony Ross

Winner of the German Children's Book Prize.

THE BOY WHO LOST HIS BELLYBUTTON
by Jeanne Willis and Tony Ross

ELIZA AND THE MOONCHILD
by Emma Chichester Clark

Shortlisted for the Booktrust Early Years Award.

SMALL
by Jessica Meserve

Shortlisted for the Cambridgeshire Children's Picture Book Award.

THE GORDON STAR
by Rebecca Patterson and Mary Rees

BOO!
by Colin McNaughton